Maria

THEODORE TAYLOR is the award-winning author of *The Cay* and its long awaited prequel/sequel, *Timothy of the Cay*. He has written more than twenty books for young readers, including *Sniper*, an ALA Best Book for Young Adults, and *The Weirdo*, winner of the 1992 Edgar Allan Poe Award. He lives with his wife Flora in a house near the ocean in Laguna Beach, California.

THEODORE TAYLOR

MARIA

A Christmas Story

AN AVON CAMELOT BOOK

The Gonzaga family, Francisco the ox, and Hernando the hinny first appeared in "The Christmas Parade," a short story by the author in *McCall's* magazine, December 1975.

AVON BOOKS
A division of
The Hearst Corporation
1350 Avenue of the Americas
New York, New York 10019

For Whitney—
beautiful, wonderful, scalawag
granddaughter

MARIA FUENTES GONZAGA

THIS EARLY OCTOBER noontime many years ago, when the farming-valley sun was still warm but the air was already autumn cool, Maria Fuentes Gonzaga listened with her teeth on edge as Eleanor Webster described her family's float for the upcoming annual Christmas parade.

". . . hundreds of white and yellow mums, white and red roses, and hundreds of poinsettias. Everything flowers. Everything. We're calling it Winter Garden. . . ."

Winter Garden? Everything flowers. White and red roses . . .

Suddenly, bottled-up envy and old anger churned

ia's brain and stomach. She wanted to clamp
ands over her ears, yell "Stop it!" at the pretty
g..., a girl.

"Same designer we had last year . . ."

Maria rubbed her palms across her skirt, straightening it. She knew the Websters' designer was from one of the big floral shops in San Francisco. She knew he charged a lot of money. But the Websters could well afford him. John Webster was a wealthy developer and cattle grower. He looked, walked, and talked wealthy.

"Oh, I forgot the orange calendulas and red poppies. . . ."

Maria didn't know what a "calendula" was and really didn't care, but she was sure that the float would be beautiful, as usual. There would be oohs and ahs from the sidelines. People watching would say, "Isn't that gorgeous!" The Websters would have done it again.

Last year, the float from their huge Mariposa Ranch, the ranch that loomed next door to the Gonzagas' meager farm like a giant, had placed second, disappointing them. Eleanor had said they were hoping for the silver trophy, the top award, this year. They'd already won it twice in the past.

And they'd likely win it again with "Winter Garden," Maria thought. Money could buy anything, she'd always heard. Her father said it frequently.

"He made a color sketch for us. Unbelievable. We saw it last night. . . ."

Maria nodded and fought back harmful words. They lurked on the tip of her tongue. Yes, money could buy anything.

For more than twenty years the town of San Lazaro, west of the Sierra Nevada in California's long, fertile San Joaquin Valley, had celebrated Christmas with a parade. There were lavish floats from businesses and large ranches and large farms. Prize horses pranced along Main Street, their riders togged out in finery. Antique carriages rolled by, smiling women in black velvet at the reins.

Bands and bell ringers from throughout the county marched and played. Santa Claus put in the required appearance, and the grand marshal was always a Hollywood celebrity. Aside from cattle and horses and farm products, the parade was San Lazaro's only real claim to fame in the San Joaquin.

The excitement began in September when contestants began to plan their floats and lasted until the first Saturday night in December. The parade was a festive event when the whole county came together on Main Street. But for some Latinos, such as eleven-year-old Maria Fuentes Gonzaga, it was a time of painful longing. No Mexican-American family or business had ever entered a float. In silence they watched and listened, then turned away as the final display went by.

"He'll bring the flowers in a truck a day ahead, then we'll work all night to place them. He already has a chart. . . ."

Maria didn't exactly know where to direct the anger; at her own people, perhaps.

The floats cost too much, she'd always been told. Seven, eight thousand dollars. Sometimes twelve or fifteen. No Latinos around San Lazaro had that kind of money to spend on a *parada*.

A few rode their horses up Main, sandwiched between the floats. Seated on silverlaced saddles, in fancy silver-buttoned outfits, wearing black sombreros, the local *caballeros* waved and smiled but seemed out of place. *Waving, smiling.*

Maria's father always shook his head when they came along. He said they were *zonzos*. Fools! Insofar as Jorge Gonzaga was concerned, it was a total *parada gringa*. Not a drop of Spanish or Indian blood was in the veins of those sitting on the floats. *Smiling, waving.*

Let them have their silly parade, he said.

Maria did not agree with her father. Main Street belonged to the Mexican-Americans as much as it belonged to the *gringos*. The parade *should* be shared.

As school-yard voices rose and fell nearby, Eleanor went on. "Now Mom and I have to figure out what to wear. She's thinking about evening gowns this year."

Last year the Websters had worn ski outfits, Maria remembered. "Snow Land" had been the theme. Real ice and snow. Mrs. Webster, with her shining teeth and ivory complexion, waved and smiled. *Waved and smiled.* Maria had carried that image home with her.

"Daddy will wear either a tuxedo or tails. So will Billy." He was Eleanor's younger brother. Tuxedos and tails probably did go with "Winter Garden," Maria thought.

Year after year she'd watched the Websters come by, waving and smiling.

She'd waved back, wanting to be up there with them.

Corliss Thomas, who was sitting opposite Maria at this lunch recess, said, "We're not sure about ours. We'll see a sketch Sunday." Their designer was from Los Angeles.

Maria repeated, vacantly, "Sunday," her thoughts somewhere else. *Why, oh, why, are we always left out?* More than half the people around San Lazaro were Mexican-Americans, yet they seemed to live in another world—their own.

Coarsegold Ranch, owned by the Thomas family, was on the other side of the Gonzagas. Sometimes the Gonzagas felt that they were indeed caught on a dab of soil between two giants. The Mariposa and the Coarsegold each spread over ten thousand acres of prime cattle land.

Jorge Gonzaga farmed exactly forty-three acres and thought he was fortunate to make a living there. He farmed them with pride.

By twelve-fifteen, Maria had had enough of the parade talk. Taking a deep breath, she said quietly, "We'll be entering Rancho Gonzaga this year."

Both Eleanor and Corliss looked at her in disbelief.

Immediately, she wanted to pull the words back out of the crisp air. What had possessed her to say them? The Gonzagas had no plans for a float. None at all.

Eleanor frowned. "You've got a small farm, Maria. Your family can't afford it."

She didn't say it meanly—rather, matter-of-factly and truthfully.

Maria replied, "Yes, we can." Even to herself, she sounded hollow. "This year, we can." What makes this year different? she thought.

Corliss Thomas asked, "Okay, what kind of float, Maria?" There was a certain dare in her voice.

"We haven't decided as yet." Maria stared at Corliss.

Corliss was just as pretty as Eleanor but not as delicate. Maria sometimes wished she had been born *gringa* blond and lived on the other side of one of the fences. Either fence.

"You've already entered?" Eleanor asked, squinting a little.

Maria hedged. "I think so."

"You better not think. The deadline's today," Corliss warned.

"I'll check when I get home."

Maria felt a rush of blood in her cheeks and forehead. Could they see it? Did the redness betray her? She thought they didn't believe her. No, she knew they didn't believe her.

"I'll check," she repeated.

Maybe that was the way out for her tomorrow. Say that the Gonzagas simply forgot about the deadline, surprising no one. A *mañana* mistake, a Mexican mistake.

Most of the time Eleanor and Corliss treated her well and were fun to be around. But she always demanded to "go Dutch" and pay her own share of anything. Gonzaga pride! It was a fact that Eleanor and Corliss seldom looked down on her because of who she was, the poor neighbor next door. But now and then, the differences—and there were many—arose.

Eleanor and Corliss lived in large, modern, one-story California-style redwood ranch houses, twelve rooms in Eleanor's, fourteen in Corliss's. Their sprawling mansions were set in gently rolling hills that were golden in summer, green in winter. Driving up to them, a visitor could see fine horses grazing or running.

Their ranches had big swimming pools. Maria was welcome to use them anytime she wanted but seldom did. Their parents drove big, new cars and shopped in San Francisco. They had their own small aircraft and landing strips.

Jorge Gonzaga had an ancient "truck," converted from a sedan, and Felicia Gonzaga, Maria's mother, had a secondhand 1951 Dodge.

Eleanor and Corliss both had honey-colored hair and got honey-colored tans and were undeniably rich *gringa* girls, but Maria, equally pretty and light mahogany in color, had never called them that out loud. She really liked them most of the time.

She added, "Whatever float we enter will be nice."

Now she had really trapped herself. *Estúpida!*

Eleanor said, "Good luck," blue eyes questioning.

Maria closed her own brown eyes, dodging Eleanor's look.

She was friendly with other Latina girls but saw

more of Eleanor and Corliss than any of the Latinas simply because of being neighbors.

Taking a deep breath, she made an excuse and left the concrete bench and table. She knew Eleanor was exactly right: the Gonzagas had a truck farm, not a *rancho*. They couldn't afford any type of float. She knew she should turn back and say, "Hey, I was just kidding." But she kept on moving away toward the school building, frustration and anger still stronger than doubt.

On the bus, going home past fields being irrigated with long silver wands of water, past crops being harvested, past tractors turning earth from brown to black, Maria sat by herself, thinking. She was again tempted to go to the girls, admit that the area's Mexican-Americans couldn't compete with the *gringos*. Maybe someday they'd be able to. Maybe never.

Yet, she suddenly thought, if everyone would chip in: The three Mexican cafés; Anaya's dry-cleaning business; Quemada's garage; the *mercado*; the grocery store owned by the Lorcas; then the farmers, even the field-workers—maybe they could have a fine float, after all.

If each would give some money? If each business owner would put a contribution bowl on the counter? And there had to be other ways—a benefit *fiesta*?

The bus pulled up at the narrow dirt road that led to her farm, Maria now concentrating on how the money might be raised. "See you tomorrow," she said to Corliss as she passed her and stepped down. Eleanor had already gotten off.

THE *DINERO* JAR

SHE TRUDGED ALONG the dusty car tracks for several hundred yards, then looked up toward the far eastern corner of their land at the figures of her father and Francisco, the massive ox. Thin dust rose up around them. They were plowing, preparing the earth for winter and spring crops. Francisco was used for heavy plowing; Hernando, their hinny, half donkey and half horse, pulled the cultivator.

Jorge Gonzaga worked their land seven days a week, only taking time off on Sunday mornings for mass at Our Lady of Guadalupe, where the masses were conducted in Spanish.

She gazed at her father and the ox a moment,

then lifted her eyes to the towering gray Sierra Nevada, mountains of strength. She often looked up at them when troubled. Finally, taking a deep breath, she went on. The serene grazing area in which they lived was known as the Jolon. In names, at least, the county was still more Spanish than *gringo*.

Her mother wasn't home as yet, she knew. Felicia did domestic chores at Coarsegold Ranch five days a week, much against the will of her husband. Jorge thought it was demeaning but didn't complain about the money she earned. She'd worked at the Coarsegold since Maria was nine. Mrs. Thomas paid well and the job was convenient enough. Two miles over the thick grasses to the Thomas house. Felicia could have walked but instead drove her old Dodge and usually arrived home about five. Maria would have preferred she didn't work for Corliss's mother.

Maria's brother, Rafael, fourteen, attended San Lazaro High and always took a later bus. He didn't arrive home until four-thirty. On days he practiced basketball, he got back around six. Anyway, talking to Rafael about entering the parade was as useless as talking to the ox.

And talking to her father about it was the last thing she wanted to do. The whole family always attended the parade. They stood on the sidelines, then went on to a Mexican café. There they discussed which float was best. But Jorge Gonzaga maintained, each year, that the parade was a waste of time. Maria often thought her father was only interested in weather; the prices of carrots, onions, peppers, beans, beets, and asparagus; and reducing his mortgage.

She reached the small, faded, yellow board-and-batten house surrounded by white oaks and blue gums a few minutes after four. For a moment she thought of calling her mother at the Thomases', saying she had a plan to enter a float in the parade and get all the Latinos around San Lazaro to make a contribution.

She knew her mother would say, "Let's talk to your father tonight." He always made the important decisions. But tonight would be too late. Talk with Jorge Gonzaga was doomed to fail, anyway. He'd say, "Are you crazy, Maria?"

She dialed the Chamber of Commerce to ask if today was the deadline. The lady said yes, five o'clock. Maria then asked if the entry fee was the same as last year—yes, twenty-five dollars. Maria knew she had five and some change in her top dresser drawer.

While on the phone she looked at her father's *dinero* jar, which rested on the window shelf above the kitchen sink. He used the money for general purposes. He didn't believe in writing checks for less than fifty dollars. Maria had never touched the money but once heard him say to her mother, "There's always twenty or thirty in there if you need it. . . ."

Thanking the Chamber of Commerce lady, she hung up and stared a while longer at the jar. She could borrow twenty from him, then ask her mother to replace it; repay her as soon as possible from baby-sitting money.

It was now four-fifteen.

Maria went outside and stood on the stoop, looking past the edge of the old tin-roofed barn in the graying light. Her father and Francisco were still plowing. At Francisco's speed, it would take them six or seven minutes to walk home if they started now.

Inside again, she stared at the jar once more, blew out a breath, then pulled the stool over to the kitchen counter. She held the jar, hesitated one last moment, then fished inside it. There were about a dozen ones and a twenty. She took the twenty.

In her small bedroom, she got her five out of the drawer and added it to the twenty.

A moment later she banged the back door shut and glanced again at the figures in the east acres. The dust was still rising. She hoped her father hadn't seen her.

The money felt hot in her hand as she began to run toward the paved county road. Though both parents had warned about hitching rides, Maria did it every so often. The four miles to San Lazaro were too far to walk.

Cars and trucks traveling past were usually driven by local people. Mr. Mendoza, from the north part of the Jolon, soon came along in his pickup, and five minutes later Maria was in town, headed for the brick Chamber of Commerce building.

Rancho Gonzaga

A BROAD-BEAMED "horse lady" in jeans and boots was at the Chamber of Commerce, talking to the girl behind the reception desk, and Maria lingered by the glass case that contained the float trophies.

For a moment, looking at them, she wavered. She realized that what she was doing was crazy, as her father would say. She was just about to turn tail and leave the building when the horse lady departed.

The young receptionist, whose nameplate read Helen Hawkins, asked, "Is there something I can do for you?"

Making a quick decision, Maria swallowed, nodded, and advanced. "I'd like to enter our ranch in the parade. . . ."

"Oh?" said Helen Hawkins. "Which ranch is that?"

"Rancho Gonzaga."

"That's one I've never heard of," she said.

"It's in the Jolon."

"Oh? Okay. The fee is twenty-five dollars."

"I have it," Maria said, extending the twenty and the five across the desk.

"Your parents sent you?" Helen Hawkins was frowning a little.

Maria understood. Here was a Mexican-American girl who couldn't be more than twelve entering a parade float. A Mexican-American float?

"They both work," Maria explained.

"Okay," said Helen Hawkins, with a shrug, sliding the form over. "Write either name in on the line that says Participant."

Maria wrote in "Jorge and Felicia Gonzaga."

"What's your theme?"

"We haven't decided yet."

"Oh, okay. Just leave that blank. Call us when you decide."

Maria nodded and filled in the address and phone number.

"We'll send you your position number and all the other information next week. Just be sure and tell your parents that the float length limit is twenty-five feet. . . ."

Maria nodded again.

Helen Hawkins said, "I'm curious. Just how large is Rancho Gonzaga?"

"It's not very large," Maria admitted.

"Cattle, horses?"

"We grow vegetables."

"Oh," said Helen Hawkins. "You know, I think this will be the first time any Mexicans have ever entered a float. How nice."

"We're Mexican-Americans," Maria said pointedly.

"Okay, all right. Mexican-Americans. The first time, though," said Helen Hawkins.

"Yes, the first time," Maria said, inhaling a shaky breath.

"Good luck," Helen Hawkins said.

Maria nodded and went out into the twilight.

On the sidewalk, she realized she was trembling all over. *She'd done it, she'd actually done it!*

After a moment, she ran in the direction where the county road intersected with Castillo and Main.

4

. . . .

FRANCISCO AND HERNANDO

MARIA ARRIVED HOME in darkness, opened the kitchen door, and immediately wished she'd stayed outside. Three pairs of suspicious eyes drilled her. They belonged to her father, her mother, and Rafael.

"Did you do it, Maria?" Jorge Gonzaga shouted.

"Do what, Papa?" That was a ridiculous question. She knew exactly what he was talking about. She'd never been able to hide guilt, anyway.

"Take twenty dollars out of the jar!"

Still standing in the doorway, Maria sighed, swallowed, and nodded. She felt awful, ashamed. Discovery was perhaps inevitable, but it was bad luck he'd found out so soon. No chance for her mother to replace the money.

Dumbfounded, Gonzaga looked at Felicia, then back to his daughter. Though she was sometimes flighty and foolish, like anyone her age, the thin, black-haired girl with the large, expressive brown eyes had always seemed so trustworthy. Now, obviously, Maria was a thief, a common sneak thief.

"Why, Maria?" her mother asked, shaking her head in disbelief.

The Gonzagas had never stolen from each other or anyone else.

"Why?" Jorge Gonzaga echoed. "Just why?"

Maria was afraid to tell him.

He glared at her. "I needed to gas up the truck and came in here a half hour ago. The twenty was gone. Why, Maria?"

Though Gonzaga seldom counted the money, he always seemed to know exactly how much was in the jar.

"Why?" he demanded again.

"I entered us in the Christmas parade, Papa," Maria said in a tiny voice, almost a whisper.

Felicia frowned.

Rafael laughed. "She's crazy."

Gonzaga's mouth dropped open. "You did what?"

He was stocky and powerful, hair the color of polished granite, skin the color of polished acorns. He'd been in the United States for thirty years, most of them spent around San Lazaro. He'd been a citizen the last fifteen years and spoke English with a soft accent.

Felicia had been born in Arizona, near the Mexican border. She'd married Jorge when he was a farmhand making a dollar an hour. He was now a self-made man and proud of it. Both Rafael and Maria were Californians, born in San Lazaro.

Maria swallowed once more and took a deep, deep breath. "I entered Rancho Gonzaga in the parade. Today was the deadline. I only had five dollars. The fee is twenty-five—"

Rafael burst into laughter again. "Rancho Gonzaga?" he mocked and walked out of the kitchen. Over his shoulder he said, *"Idiota!"*

Maria winced. She and Rafael were always at war. They'd been at war as long as she could remember. Rafael waged war with words.

"Oh my," Felicia said. She turned back to the stove.

Gonzaga sat down heavily at the kitchen table near her. "A float from Rancho Gonzaga, eh?" he said, staring at his daughter. "Are you insane? They would laugh us off the street. We have a poor little truck farm here, not a *rancho*. You know that, Maria. We raise vegetables, not cattle or horses. Why did you do it without asking me?

Maria took yet another deep breath. It was very hard to explain. It was always hard to explain anything to him. When angry, he was like a volcano. "We were all in the school yard at lunch today—"

" 'We'?" Gonzaga exploded.

Felicia returned to the table, wooden stirring spoon in hand, and looked at her daughter with concern. She was a gentle woman and said, "Ssssh," to her husband to calm him down.

"Eleanor and Corliss were talking about their floats. Eleanor said theirs would have real flowers, and Corliss said their designer was coming Sunday to show them a sketch. I felt left out, as usual, Papa. I said we'd have one too. . . ."

Gonzaga grunted and sighed.

"Then Eleanor said we couldn't afford it. I got angry, came home, and took the money out of your jar. I'll pay you back, I promise."

His own anger beginning to ebb, Gonzaga said tiredly, "You should have asked me. I would have told you we cannot compete with these people. It takes much money, Maria. The big ranchers have it. The gas company has it; the automobile dealers have it; the power company has it. We do not. Tomorrow, after school, go straight to the Chamber of Commerce and tell them you made a mistake."

Tears swiftly filled Maria's eyes. "What will I say at school?"

"Tell them I decided not to enter the parade after all. Blame it on me," her father said, sighing again.

Maria fought the tears. She was always fighting something. "I thought we could get our own people to contribute to the float. The Quemadas, the Lorcas . . ."

Gonzaga scoffed. "They have no more interest in it than I do."

Maria fled to her bedroom, hearing her father say

to her mother, "She should not have done it, you know that."

Felicia followed Maria and sat down by her to say the old litany soothingly, "I know what it is to be left out. It happened to me many times when I was your age."

Maria wrenched herself up from the bed and ran through the kitchen, past her father, and out into the yard, fighting back sobs.

She moved aimlessly around the yard for a moment, feeling devastated, then went into the barn, where Francisco and Hernando were still feeding. In times past, after a bad day they had been of comfort. They were big and warm. Sniffling, she slumped down in hay near the wide doors and looked at them in the shadows.

Last year she'd done a school paper on them. Oxen were bull cattle that had been fixed so they couldn't produce offspring. They didn't act like bulls anymore. Powerful Francisco, who was twelve years old, was as gentle as a rabbit. He'd learned to follow Gonzaga's simple plowing and walking commands. He was white, with big black blotches.

Mules were offspring of male donkeys and female

horses. Hernando was the son of a female donkey and a stallion—a hinny. All hinnies were considered to be inferior to mules. Hernando had long ears, a tufted tail, and slender legs. His bray was loud but he wasn't temperamental, like most donkeys and mules.

Everyone had laughed in class when she read her paper about Francisco and Hernando. She'd felt foolish, knowing she should have written about something else. Another Maria mistake.

Now she stared at the animals. Why her father had to have a ridiculous ox, she'd never know. If he couldn't afford a tractor like other farmers, why couldn't he at least have a couple of ordinary mules? Sluggish Francisco—she didn't believe there was another ox in the whole county; maybe not anywhere in the whole state of California. Everyone laughed at the strange pair of animals, she knew. Well, they deserved to be laughed at.

Beyond that, people were laughing at the Jorge Gonzagas. A year ago she'd loved these animals. Now she almost hated the sight of them. They represented all Mexicans who couldn't afford tractors, much less floats.

Suddenly, she raged at Hernando. "You're not even a pure donkey. You're stupid!" The hinny rotated his head slightly to look at her with soft, loving eyes. "So are you stupid, Francisco!"

The ox gave her a look that might have held surprise.

Then Maria heard her mother calling her to dinner. She dabbed at the moisture on her cheeks and went into the house, sitting down stiffly at the table. The family did not speak very much during the meal.

Maria went straight to her room after washing the dishes. It was up to Rafael to dry them.

She heard her mother say. "It is *orgullo*. Pure pride."

Her father answered, "I know the meaning of *orgullo* as much as you do, as much as anybody. But she did a foolish thing and now she has to pay in pride."

5

THE EXCUSE

DURING THE NIGHT, Maria hoped that morning would never come. It did, of course, and at breakfast her mother said, "Papa will take you to the Chamber of Commerce this afternoon." His workday with Francisco and Hernando had begun an hour earlier.

"Will they give our money back?"

"I don't know," Felicia said. "That's why he's going with you."

Maria went silently off to school, dreading it. She avoided Rafael as they walked down the road by the wire fencing to the bus stop. But he taunted her from behind. "Where's our Rancho Gonzaga sign?"

She stood away from him at the stop. His bus always came first. She was relieved when it drew up and went off in a torrent of exhaust.

In the sleepless hours she'd rehearsed what she planned to say to Corliss Thomas and Eleanor Webster: "Papa decided we wouldn't have a float, after all. He can't take the time away from planting." Her father worked the year round. The winter crop was carrots. Although there could be a few weeks when the weather was cold and raw, when fog covered the valley, the ground never froze.

Under no circumstances would she admit to them that she'd actually entered Rancho Gonzaga yesterday and would be withdrawing it today. Never would she tell them that she'd swiped twenty dollars from her father. They probably got that much each in weekly allowances.

The bus finally came along and Maria boarded it, moving up the aisle to sit down beside Corliss, who had a red bow in her hair to match the red sweater she was wearing.

Even before the driver meshed gears and the bus began to move, Corliss asked about the parade.

Maria shook her head and told Corliss the excuse she'd rehearsed. There was some truth in it. Jorge Gonzaga really didn't have time to decorate a float. Maria didn't mention the money problem. During the night she had realized it would take months to raise enough money from the Latino families—if they ever could raise it. Maria also realized the whole thing had indeed been dumb, as Rafael had said. She hadn't thought it out.

A few minutes later Eleanor climbed aboard. She asked the same question, and Maria gave the same answer: winter planting.

Corliss and Eleanor exchanged looks that said, *Just what we thought.* The Mexican-American neighbors couldn't hack it.

Corliss said, "Too bad. Maybe next year, huh?"

Maria nodded, swallowing defeat.

"You can help dress ours," Eleanor offered. Helpers were always needed to place the flowers the night before the parade.

Maria nodded again.

Throughout the day she was listless and down, and it wasn't from lack of sleep. What she'd done was dumb, all right. But admitting it to herself didn't lessen the pain. That sting remained even after the final bell rang.

6

THE DECISION

JORGE GONZAGA WAS still in his work clothes—stained, faded corduroy jacket, worn jeans, muddy boots, straw hat—when she arrived home. For a moment she thought of suggesting he change to his Sunday clothes to visit the Chamber of Commerce. Then she decided that wouldn't be wise. People in San Lazaro were accustomed to seeing farm workers in worn jeans and muddy boots fresh from the fields.

A few minutes later she slid into the vehicle her father called a truck. It wasn't a truck at all. It was a battered, rusting four-door Ford sedan, backseat removed. He'd cut the body off behind the driver's seat. It hauled hampers of vegetables, sacks of fertilizer, and tools. Maria was ashamed to ride in it. The truck was in the same category as Francisco and Hernando.

"When I get the mortgage paid off, I'll buy a real truck," her father had promised. He usually meant what he said. Mortgage first, even if it took twenty years.

As they turned left on the county road and headed for San Lazaro, he said, "You ask for the money back and I'll say to her, 'Blame it on me.' Okay?"

That much was right. He *was* to blame. More than he knew. "Okay," she said.

He said, "Talk to me before you do something like this again. . . ."

Same old Papa. "You would have said no."

"Give me the chance to say no. I'm not as bad as you think."

Yes, you are, she thought. *You are a stubborn, penny-pinching dictator and you'll never change.*

At the first stoplight on Main, a shiny white pickup came up alongside them and Maria attempted to disappear in her seat. The timing couldn't have been worse.

"Mr. Mariposa" himself, Albert Webster, Eleanor's father, shouted over, "Hey, Gonzaga, I hear you're putting in a float this year." Eleanor hadn't had time to tell him differently.

A distinguished, handsome man in a white Stetson hat, he grinned widely at the Gonzagas. Maria thought he meant no ill will but could feel her father's tension, see it in his knuckles on the gearshift.

Gonzaga looked over at the ruddy-faced rancher. Maria knew he'd never particularly liked Webster, though they hadn't had any trouble as neighbors. Webster had made some halfhearted attempts to buy the scant Gonzaga acres. She'd seen and heard her father refuse. With a smile.

"What kinda float you gonna put in, Gonzaga?" Webster asked with amiable curiosity. "They cost a lot, I tell you. I should know."

Perhaps it was advice, perhaps something else? Maria felt her pulse quicken. There was that *orgullo* again, stabbing her. The old wounds opened.

Her father agreed. "Yes, they do cost a lot, I've heard." He said it calmly but she knew his temper was simmering. Maria saw his hand tighten on the gearshift.

Webster said seriously, "Tell you what, Gonzaga. You really need a designer if you plan to compete. That's for certain. I'll give you mine. Florist over in San Francisco. But I'll warn you, he's expensive."

Gonzaga continued to look at Webster but didn't answer.

Maria guessed what the rancher was thinking: *Hah, leave it to Gonzaga and he'll probably have a giant tortilla for a float. Maybe a mound of refried beans?*

Jorge Gonzaga finally nodded as the light changed. "I'll let you know, Mr. Webster."

Webster waved good-bye and the new truck pulled ahead, gliding away. Sun gleamed on the chrome.

Gonzaga glanced at Maria. "The whole valley probably knows you entered us by now."

"Maybe," she admitted. Not maybe! Of course they knew. There were a lot of gossips around San Lazaro. Anything unusual traveled from lip to ear in no time. Latinos in the Christmas parade were news. Big news.

Soon, Gonzaga parked in front of the Chamber building, and Maria followed him inside, preparing to do as instructed: cancel and ask for return of the fee. Do it quickly, and get out.

She noticed that he paused at the glass case holding the silver trophy, but he said nothing. He stared at the trophy a long time.

Moving on, her father spoke first. "Please, who is in charge here?"

The same girl who had accepted the entry yesterday was behind the desk. Puzzled, Helen Hawkins looked at Maria and asked Gonzaga, "What do you want to know?"

"My name is Jorge Gonzaga and my daughter was here yesterday." He glanced over at Maria.

Helen Hawkins smiled at the man in worn jeans, muddy boots, and straw hat. "And now you want your money back?"

"Oh, no," Gonzaga said quickly. "I came by to sign papers."

Maria frowned. Had she heard right? Did he say "*sign papers*"?

Helen Hawkins frowned, too. "Your daughter signed yesterday. As I told her, we'll mail your parade number and the instructions next week. Limit your float to twenty-five feet."

"Okay, then. Rancho Gonzaga will be in the parade. That is definite."

Maria felt her body lifting off the earth like a rocket as the frowning girl said, "Good luck," but her father was already moving toward the door.

Out on the sidewalk, Maria yelled, "You changed your mind, Papa! You changed your mind!" and ran into his arms.

He grinned at her. "I'm as crazy as you are."

. . . .

7

WHAT KIND OF FLOAT?

ALMOST THE MOMENT they entered the faded yellow house, Maria smiling widely, Gonzaga declared to Felicia, "I am now the biggest *zonzo* in the county."

"Why do you say that?" she asked.

"Because I just told the Chamber of Commerce that Rancho Gonzaga will definitely be in the parade."

Felicia gasped, then began to laugh. "I don't believe it."

"He did," Maria said. "He did, Mama."

Felicia kissed her husband and embraced him. "Why did you change your mind?"

• 39 •

"I don't know, I don't know," he said, shaking his head, laughing softly at his own weakness.

Maria knew why—that *orgullo* they all wrestled with, that pride that made them cry, made them fight, made them do foolish things.

Rafael, a little later, wasn't too enthused. He as much as said he wanted nothing to do with it. But that was Rafael, as usual, Maria thought. Anything Maria was for, he was against. She shrugged. So what! If it had been *his* idea, he would have joined the celebration.

At supper, Felicia asked Gonzaga what kind of float he intended to build. Both Maria and Rafael awaited his answer.

"I'll have to think about it," he said uncertainly, even uncomfortably.

"It'll be a beautiful float, won't it?" said Maria. "Even if we don't win, it'll be a beautiful float, won't it?"

Already, she was anxiously thinking about the other floats, especially those entered by the Thomases and the Websters.

Her father nodded, casting a sudden concerned look at her mother as if he hadn't thought, at all, about that part—the building of the float. What was going to be on it?

"Yes, it will be beautiful. Everyone will help," Felicia said.

"Everyone?" Gonzaga asked, bushy eyebrows raised.

"All our friends."

"I hope," he murmured. It appeared he was having second thoughts.

For a few minutes there were only the sounds of forks and spoons scraping chinaware, the ticking of the kitchen clock. Then Rafael asked, "Don't you have *any* ideas?" He was looking at his father.

"No," said Gonzaga, glumly. "Give me some time."

"Maria?" Rafael said, seeming to enjoy the fact that they had no ideas.

After a moment of thought, Maria said, "I'll find that picture book of the Rose Parade." They'd gone to Pasadena to see it the year before.

"Those floats cost a hundred thousand dollars," Rafael scoffed.

"Or more," Gonzaga said ruefully.

"Mother?" Rafael asked.

"We might get some friends together and have a *fiesta* scene. Sing and dance . . ."

Gonzaga said, "Felicia, that would take a float forty feet long, and the limit is twenty-five."

"We'll think of something," she said.

"Just remember I don't have a tractor." Most of the floats were pulled by tractors, though some of the business floats had engines built into them.

"You could rent one," Maria suggested.

He gave her a negative look. "I have better things to do with our money."

Maria said, "I'll start tomorrow and ask for contributions, put jars on the store counters. . . ."

"You'll do no such thing!" her father said, alarmed, his voice rising. "If anyone wants to volunteer a donation, okay. Don't ask for *anything*. Understand? That's an order!"

Disappointed, Maria nodded. She had been certain many of the Latinos would be glad to give money.

Before the meal ended, it was clearly evident that Jorge Gonzaga now regretted his impulsive decision at the Chamber of Commerce. By bedtime, he was furious with himself as well as with everyone else.

Before he went off to bed at his usual eight-thirty, he announced firmly, "We have a budget of ten dollars."

Felicia's mouth opened, speechless for a few seconds. Finally, she said, "You can't do *anything* with ten dollars. Anything."

Maria said, "Papa . . ." She was stricken.

"I'll take a hundred out of my savings," Felicia said.

"Ten dollars is what we'll spend," Gonzaga said, nodding grimly. "That's all. Ten!"

As soon as the bedroom door closed with finality, Maria appealed to her mother.

"You heard what he said. It means no parade. . . ."

"We'll try," said Felicia, but the expression on her face offered little hope.

A moment later Gonzaga stalked out of the bedroom, barefoot in his long winter underwear. "We'll have a display of vegetables. Carrots, peppers, beans . . ."

Maria was horrified and Rafael laughed.

Felicia both laughed and sighed. "Jorge, carrots and peppers don't represent Christmas. . . ."

He stalked silently back into his bedroom, and Maria went to hers in tears.

THE MARIACHI MAN

NEXT MORNING, A sparkling Saturday, the phone rang at the Gonzagas' and Felicia said, "It's for you, Maria."

Eleanor Webster said, "Daddy told me you decided to enter a float, after all. That's great."

"Yes," Maria said.

"You don't sound happy about it."

"Oh, I am," Maria said, though the tone of her voice was anything but happy.

"Your father changed his mind?"

"He'll take some time off next month to build it." Maria knew she sounded lifeless. She felt that way.

"I'll tell Corliss. We'll both help you if you need us."

"Thanks."

"Okay. What are you planning?"

"We're not sure," Maria said. What could you plan with ten dollars to spend?

"Well, it sneaks up on you. Just ask Daddy. Seven weeks from tonight."

"Daddy" Webster was one person who wouldn't be asked under any circumstances. At least, not by Jorge Gonzaga.

"We'll know soon," said Maria. One way or another, she thought, we'll know soon.

"I hope so," said Eleanor. "You wanna ride this afternoon?"

The Websters had seven or eight horses, of which three were gentle. Riding back into the foothills was fun, and Maria usually went whenever invited. "Think I'll pass. I'm not feeling so hot."

"Take some aspirin. See you Monday," Eleanor said and hung up.

Felicia had overheard the conversation. "The world isn't coming to an end," she advised.

"I hate Papa for being so stingy," Maria said angrily.

"He is just careful where money is concerned," Felicia said, "and anyway that doesn't solve the problem."

As her father had predicted, the word had spread.

In the days that followed, some foggy, gray, and chill, others sunny and chill—typical November days for that part of the San Joaquin—Maria thought that every Mexican-American in the whole valley had found a way to get in touch with the Gonzagas and ask about the float.

Gonzaga was asked at the wholesale market; Felicia was asked wherever she went. Rafael was asked at the high school, and Maria found herself dodging the question in the hallways, in class, and every other place she stood or sat still a moment. The Panadero girl asked and the Anaya girl asked, as did the Villarreal and Villaseñor boys; Juan Paz asked and Juan Cruz asked and Lily Cisneros asked. Ten or twenty others, at least.

Some people even dropped by the farm to find out what the Gonzagas were doing.

Finally, one night, Jorge blew up. "You would think I've been appointed to represent all of them!" he shouted. "But do they offer money? No! Do they give me ideas? No! They simply ask what I'm going to do. 'Hey, Gonzaga, what about the float? Will *we* win?' "

He waved a fist in the air and roared, " '*We*'!"

He was in the kitchen that evening. Maria had never seen him so frustrated or angry. His face was as red as his beets. She thought he might have a heart attack.

Felicia said, "Calm down, Jorge. They're just curious. They mean well."

He sat down heavily and looked up accusingly at Maria. "Look what you got us into. . . ."

Her mother quietly reminded him that he'd made the final decision. Maria again felt guilty, nonetheless.

On a foggy evening in mid-November, a *mariachi* man named Rodolfo Galarza drove up to pay a visit unannounced. Most everyone in the valley around San Lazaro knew Rodolfo. His band had played at parties and other functions for years. It was a good *mariachi* group, and his men always wore the traditional costume.

Gonzaga offered him a beer, and Rodolfo sat at the kitchen table, the usual place visitors were entertained. He said, "Jorge, the word is that you're in trouble. You don't know what to put on your float."

Maria listened intently, having a hunch what was about to happen.

Her father answered, "I'm not in trouble at all. I just haven't decided."

Rodolfo said, "The parade is three weeks away."

"I know that," Gonzaga said.

"I'll tell you what. Put my band up on your float. I'll cut the price in half. I usually charge two hundred fifty. We'll play for you for a hundred twenty-five."

Maria could tell by the look on her father's face that he was tempted.

"That's a lot of money, Rodolfo," he said.

"For eleven men? Ten dollars each for the others, and twenty-five for me?"

Her father rubbed his chin.

Felicia said, "Why don't we think about it? We don't have to make the decision tonight."

"Well, that is a busy period and maybe someone else will book us," Rodolfo said, looking over at her.

"Yes, why don't we think about it," said Gonzaga.

Maria let out a breath of relief.

Rodolfo finished his beer and departed.

As the beams of his headlights, backing away, flashed over the house, Maria said, "If he plays I'd rather not have a float at all."

"Why not?" her father asked, glancing at her.

Maria said, "Everyone has heard Rodolfo many times." That was true. He'd played next door for the Thomases' Fourth of July party. She'd helped her mother serve that night. He'd also played at every *fiesta* she could remember.

"He can play carols," Gonzaga said.

Rafael arrived home from basketball practice, having been dropped off at the road, and asked, "Who was that?" Rodolfo's car had passed him.

"Rodolfo Galarza. I'm thinking about using his *mariachis* for the float," Gonzaga said.

"Good idea," Rafael said.

"Please don't, Papa," Maria said.

Gonzaga looked angrily from his daughter to his wife, then back to his daughter. "This has gone on long enough," he said, fuming. "It's Rodolfo or I'll eat my pride, along with yours and that of every other stingy, ungrateful Mexican in this valley. It's Rodolfo or I'll go to the Chamber of Commerce and tell them we withdraw. . . ."

Felicia said, "If you gave us more than ten dollars, maybe we could—"

Gonzaga interrupted with a shout and jumped up, sending his chair sprawling. "We *withdraw*, we *withdraw!*"

9

THE OX AND THE HINNY

MARIA FLED OUTSIDE. Dry-eyed, she was as weary of it as they were. Maybe it was best to cancel, for everyone's sake. Swallow bitter *orgullo* no matter how much it hurt. She walked aimlessly around the barnyard.

The cold on her face and hands felt good. A full moon was out, lighting the lonely, still countryside. The moonlight reflected off the snow peaks of the Sierras, making them appear as white clouds floating above the dark slopes. Moonlight made the silent Jolon beautiful.

Finally, at peace with herself, she entered the barn and sat down opposite the stalls of Francisco and Hernando.

Shafts of the soft light lay across the straw and animals. She looked at them a long time and then thought, *Navidad*. Yes, *Navidad*. Why hadn't she thought of it before? Why hadn't anyone thought of it? So simple, so easy.

She rushed back into the kitchen. "I know what to do."

"About what?" her mother asked.

"The float. Where is the Bible?"

"In our bedroom."

Maria followed her mother into the bedroom, where Gonzaga was sprawled out on top of the covers, head cupped in his hands, staring at the ceiling. He didn't bother to look at either of them.

They returned to the kitchen, and Maria leafed through the pages of the old, thick, illustrated Spanish Bible. She remembered that toward the back was a painting of the Nativity. "There," she said, glancing at her mother.

Part of the stable appeared to be built in a cave. A donkey was visible, as was a cow. Maria said happily, "That's what we can do. Without the cave. Why didn't we think of it before? It'll cost Papa nothing."

Looking over her shoulder, Felicia said approvingly, "It's wonderful, Maria."

She rousted Gonzaga from the bed, telling him of Maria's idea.

They got a flashlight and returned to the barn, comparing the painting with their own mismatched animals. "You see," said Gonzaga, as if the idea were his own, "we have everything, even to Hernando. We won't have to spend a dollar."

They returned to the house.

Rafael was still in the kitchen.

"Here it is," said Gonzaga to Rafael, grinning. "Look, our float!" His thick finger pointed to the figures in the painting. "Your sister will be Mary. You'll be Joseph. I'll build part of the barn on the old flatbed wagon. Hernando will be here." His finger tapped. "Francisco will tow it. . . ."

Rafael said, "Saint Catherine's always has that float. The *mariachis* will be better."

"Why not two *Navidades?*" Felicia asked sensibly. "The other one will not look like ours. They have no animals. Ours will be real."

Rafael groaned. "Everyone will laugh at Hernando and Francisco. Then they'll laugh at us.

Dumb Mexicans with their dumb animals. Whose idea was this?"

"Maria's," said Felicia.

"You might know," said Rafael, sighing.

Maria stood by silently. Maybe Rafael was right. Maybe it was another idea she hadn't thought out.

Gonzaga eyed his son. "I don't think so. I am a farmer. These are our helpers. They help me feed us. And you will be a handsome Joseph."

Rafael looked more like his mother than his father. He was tall and slender.

Glaring at all of them, Rafael said, "I don't want to be Joseph and ride on the dumb flatbed. Every kid I know'll be laughing at me. . . ."

Gonzaga raged at Rafael. "This is what we will do. I want no more talk about it. Not a word. *Silencio!*"

The next morning, he personally called the Chamber of Commerce to announce that the theme of the Rancho Gonzaga float was a secret.

"Oh, that's original," said Helen Hawkins, laughing. "I'll put that down—'A secret.'"

Gonzaga held his temper.

10

THE SECRET

GONZAGA SWORE THEM all to secrecy. "Since no one has volunteered to help or give money, we will tell no one. No one at all. We will show no one."

"You can't see it until that night," Maria soon said to Eleanor and Corliss.

"No one's float is ever a surprise," Eleanor said.

"Ours will be," Maria answered, on orders of her father.

Some surprise! Millions of Nativity scenes had been built around the world and they all looked much the same. Maria felt they should go ahead and tell everyone what the Rancho Gonzaga "secret" really was: they didn't have enough money. Yet it wasn't worth another fight with Jorge Gonzaga.

One of the Panadero boys was caught sneaking around the barn, looking through a window. Gonzaga threatened him with a pitchfork, though there was nothing to be seen in the barn as yet.

Rafael had barely spoken to Maria since the night he'd been selected to be Joseph. He blamed it all on her.

In the kitchen a week later, he yelled, "I won't do it! I'm not going to do it. Get somebody else. . . ."

Only Maria and her mother were there. Gonzaga was plowing.

"You don't need to yell," said Felicia.

"I'm telling you, they'll laugh and point at me. . . ." He meant kids from San Lazaro High.

"They might not," his mother said, but she knew they would. So did Maria.

Though she wouldn't admit it, Maria had begun to feel that some kind of disaster would happen on Main Street. She had no idea what it would be, but nothing had gone right so far. Maybe her brother would jump down and run off into the night? Maybe a wheel would come off the flatbed midway along the route? Maybe Francisco would decide to poop just as they passed the judges' stand? She didn't share her fears out loud.

Rafael shouted, "I won't do it!" and stalked out, slamming the door to his room.

Felicia looked after him.

Maria said, "He always pulls that when Papa isn't here."

Her mother nodded.

Yet Maria did feel a little sorry for him. Fourteen-year-old boys, ones who played football, basketball, and baseball, didn't want to dress like Joseph in public.

On the last day of November, Gonzaga began to build the Nativity scene in his spare time. The big-wheeled flatbed had been used for many things around the farm. Gonzaga had bought it second-hand years ago. Dings and bruises, cuts and scrapes, and stains of mashed vegetables were all evident.

Baling wire held some of the boards together. It even smelled of the farm.

After Gonzaga towed the flatbed inside the barn, hiding it, Maria took a close look. The feeling of dread returned. "Do you think it'll make it?" she asked.

"Of course it will. It is not a thing of beauty, but it is strong. You see floats break down in parades. There is nothing to break here," her father said.

The tops of the thick boards in the bed were shredded in places. "Can we cover them?" she asked.

"With what?"

"A sheet or something."

He pointed to the painting in the Bible that rested nearby. "Do you see sheets there?"

There was earth and straw.

Maria thought it might be best not to come out here again; she would wait until he'd finished.

"I'm going to strip some boards off the barn and remove part of the feed trough for the manger. It will look real, Maria. I promise." The weathered boards were at least fifty years old.

As she departed, she heard him telling Francisco and Hernando what was expected of them.

She knew that whatever project stubborn Jorge Gonzaga undertook he went all the way, right or wrong.

Meanwhile, Felicia was busy at her sewing machine. Spending less than five dollars of the ten her husband had allotted, she made a white robe for Maria, an exact copy of the painting. She made a striped robe of coarse cloth for Rafael. She made a headdress from a towel and converted an old robe for Gonzaga's costume.

Rafael took one look at his and went into a rage.

THE ROAD TO SAN LAZARO

ABOUT NOON, ON the first Saturday in December, Maria helped her father hose down Francisco and Hernando. Then she curried both of them.

To Francisco, she said, "Pull steadily, as you have always done."

To Hernando, she said, "Do not bray while you are on the wagon." Though he was half horse, Hernando's bray was formidable. "Just eat. That is all. Make us proud of you."

She still felt that disaster approached. It hovered like a bird of prey. Francisco and Hernando had seldom left the peaceful acres. Maybe they'd panic and bolt at the tractor noises and confusion, the blaring trumpets of the bands. Hernando had once jumped the Websters' fence and run two miles after her mother's car backfired. Maria would say her Hail Marys, then hold her breath and pray until the parade was over.

The Chamber's instructions said that all floats must be in position at the east end of Main Street by six P.M., and shortly after three, Gonzaga hitched Francisco to the flatbed, tying Hernando behind.

In jeans, a blouse, and a jacket, Maria walked with her father. She knew she could climb aboard whenever she wanted during the painfully slow four miles. Francisco was strong and wouldn't mind her weight, though he was not built for speed.

Rafael was playing basketball at the school gym and would join them, Maria hoped, at the east end of Main. Felicia would drive to town with their robes about five-thirty.

The "secret" was out. As they moved along the county road, cars and trucks slowed and went around them, occupants staring at the odd sight of an ox pulling a flatbed on which a flimsy barn section had been built, a queer-looking donkey walking behind it. It was a ridiculous sight.

Maria knew some were laughing.

One of Gonzaga's friends came by and shouted, "Hey, Jorge, the *burro* looks like you."

Gonzaga raised a finger. He was in no mood for jokes.

Maria knew that Eleanor and Corliss, in their expensive costumes, would be driven into town to take their places on the family floats. She hoped the flatbed would arrive long before that happened.

They reached San Lazaro about five-fifteen, darkness having fallen, streetlights on. Both were immediately tempted to turn around, slip away home in the safety of the night. The other floats were things of beauty, particularly Rancho Mariposa's garden of fresh flowers. Maria was glad to see that the Websters' number was sixteen, well behind the Gonzagas' ninth position.

The Thomases' Coarsegold float, two huge white stallions made of petals, was twelfth. The stallions were seven or eight feet tall.

Looking at them, Gonzaga said, shaking his head,

"The money they spent could feed us for two years."

"We tried, Papa," Maria said. The quicker it began and ended, the better for everyone. Rafael came up out of the shadows, looked at the other floats and then at Rancho Gonzaga's. Staring at her angrily, he said, "You happy now?"

Maria didn't answer.

Soon, Felicia arrived with the robes. As she stepped out of the car, Gonzaga, forcing himself to be cheerful, walked over to her. "Everything is fine," he said. "You see, the night is beginning to help us." The flatbed needed all the help it could get.

Felicia, surveying the other floats, said, with a slight grimness, "Ours is different. That's good. You'll be beautiful, Maria. So will you, Rafael."

Neither answered.

Maria shivered in the early evening chill, and her father said, "Stay in the car until I call you. You, too, Rafael." They were only too glad to escape.

As they walked away, Gonzaga put on his robe and headdress. Maria heard him joke feebly with her mother. "I look like an Arab."

In a few minutes an official walked over to tell

Gonzaga that the floats were beginning to line up and that he should move up the street to his proper place. Mercifully, the official made no comment about the Rancho Gonzaga entry.

Gonzaga then led Hernando up a ramp onto the flatbed and led Francisco a half block to get into ninth position, between a fine float sponsored by the Bank of America and one entered by California Edison. It was obvious that both floats had been designer built.

He lit the lantern that would cast an orange glow over Maria and the manger. Her first childhood doll was the Christ Child, wrapped in swaddling clothes.

Just before six, Felicia returned to the car to get Maria and Rafael. Sitting in the far corners of the backseat, dressed in their robes, they had not spoken in twenty minutes. Maria had thought she knew all the cruel words Rafael was capable of, but she had heard a few more this night.

A moment later, they climbed up warily to take their places beside the manger.

Felicia said to them, with some fierceness, "Whatever anyone thinks, our own people will know we tried. They will applaud us, I'm sure."

Gonzaga nodded tensely. "I plan to look straight ahead, close my ears to what anyone says and keep moving." But he appeared ready to fight any man who laughed.

Finally, Gonzaga and Felicia stepped back to look at their float and were suddenly overwhelmed. The evening shadows made the scene almost a duplicate of the painting in their Bible. Only the cow was missing. Under lantern light, it was breathtakingly real, even to Hernando munching on alfalfa in the trough near the Christ Child.

Almost in tears, Felicia said to Maria, "I wish you could see yourself. You're beautiful. Just look down at Him. Stay still."

Maria, sensing what had happened, said, "I feel beautiful, I do."

Even Rafael had noticed what the night and the lantern light had done to the float. His sour look had vanished. "How am I?"

Gonzaga studied his son. "You are fine. You're both fine." Then he moved to stand by Francisco, crossing his heart and looking up at the heavens for help.

12

. . . .

THE PARADE

PROMPTLY AT SIX, the first band began to play and the Gonzagas heard a long blast on a whistle. Gonzaga waited until the float ahead began to move, then he said to Francisco, "We go now."

The ox stayed absolutely motionless.

Gonzaga had had other such experiences, though they had been infrequent. He said calmly, "Francisco, now we go," and grasped the handmade headstall.

Francisco paid not the slightest attention. There was laughter from the sidelines. The funny Mexican was having trouble with his ox, surprising no one.

Gonzaga kept his voice down. He said in Spanish, "Why are you doing this to me? We must go."

"Move!" he shouted in English. But Francisco did not budge. The laughter grew.

Gonzaga glanced back at Maria and Rafael. They looked demolished.

Maria sat stiffly above the Christ Child. Her eyes were closed, and her hands were in fists.

Again in Spanish, Gonzaga snarled at Francisco, "You are disgracing us," and turned to drive a fist into the animal's heavy shoulder. The ox promptly sat down between the shafts, and the laughter of the crowd grew to a roar. The Gonzagas wanted to vanish. Tears shimmered in Maria's eyes.

The Bank of America float was now a half block up the street, and a parade official wheeled over on his motorbike to shout, "Get going, or we're going around you. . . ."

In an anguished voice, Gonzaga said, "I am trying," as he attempted to tug Francisco erect. But the ox had made up his mind not to move. Divine powers would not have straightened his rear legs.

The parade began to move on. California Edison's "Dream of Christmas" circled out, followed by float eleven, the Del Monte Company's entry. Soon, the huge white-flower stallions of Coarsegold Ranch passed by. Corliss Thomas, in her riding outfit, looked over in sympathy.

Felicia ran up to comfort Maria, who was now weeping openly. Rafael stood on the flatbed as if frozen, disgraced.

The best and loudest show in town was still in the number nine position as Jorge Gonzaga pleaded with Francisco to cooperate. Then he cursed him, oaths flying out over the peaceful barn of Bethlehem.

At first there was only a trickle of faces toward the stranded flatbed, but then they began to increase in numbers as the Panaderos, the Castillos, the Lorcas, the Garcias and Anayas, the Valdezes, and many more gathered to advise and help their fellow countryman.

Until the day he died, Jorge Gonzaga did not know who said, "Unhitch that silly ox and get him out of here." But having no better solution, Gonzaga quickly relieved Francisco of his pulling duties. The ox came willingly.

It was Felicia who whispered to her husband, "Our friends are going to pull the wagon."

Then Maria called down, "Papa, put Francisco up here beside Hernando."

Gonzaga was in such a helpless state that he complied without much thought and ramped Francisco up to where he wanted to be, where he always was this time of night—beside Hernando, munching feed.

The painting in the old Spanish Bible was now complete.

With twenty men on the shafts, the Arab-robed farmer walking proudly at the head, the float of Rancho Gonzaga began to move along the main street of San Lazaro.

Then a man named Guerrero, who had brought a guitar with him because he had to play at a café later that night, walked by the float, and Maria called out to him, "Please sing a carol."

In a clear, strong voice, walking ahead of Jorge Gonzaga, he began to sing, "Away in a Manger."

His words carried into the starry sky above, and a certain magic proceeded along with the wheels of the old flatbed.

No one in the county had ever seen a Nativity quite like it. Proud, solemn-faced men, instead of noisy tractors, were pulling the float. A hinny and an ox were on it. The section of the barn truly looked as if it might have come from Bethlehem. The crowds along the street became quiet as the Rancho Gonzaga float approached, heralded by the caroler.

Within a few blocks, it was evident that the humble had swept aside the grand.

And the smile on the face of Maria Fuentes Gonzaga, as she looked down at the Christ Child, told a story in itself.

To those who travel California's San Joaquin Valley in the month of December, it is worth an hour on the first Saturday evening to see the San Lazaro Christmas parade and the traditional Mexican-American Nativity scene, pulled by twenty solemn men in straw hats and overalls. Jorge and his good wife, Felicia, have passed away, as have Francisco and Hernando, but the Rancho Gonzaga entry, with the same section of weathered barn, a cow and a donkey on it, moves along as if they were all still alive.

The youngest son of Rafael is now Joseph, and the tall man who proudly walks out in front of the Silver Trophy float, singing "Away in a Manger," is Rafael himself.

Maria? Maria? She stands on the sidelines smiling at her youngest daughter, now the Virgin Mary. As pretty Blanca passes by on the old flatbed, Maria sees herself and remembers again that other magic night long ago.